PRINCE JAKE

He's the Prince of Pranks!

It's Snow Joke!

FOR LISSY, JAMES AND DANIEL
BROTHWELL, WITH LOTS OF LOVE
S.M.

FOR MY SISTER, JANET
M.B.

ORCHARD BOOKS
338 Euston Road, London NW1 3BH
Orchard Books Australia
Level 17/205 Kent St, Sydney, NSW 2000

First published in 2008 by Orchard Books
First paperback publication in 2009
Text © Sue Mongredien 2008
Illustrations © Mark Beech 2008

ISBN HB 978 1 40830 277 4
ISBN PB 978 1 84616 614 3

1 3 5 7 9 10 8 6 4 2
Printed in Great Britain by
CPI Cox & Wyman, Reading, RG1 8EX

Orchard Books is a division of Hachette Children's Books
an Hachette Livre UK company.
www.hachettelivre.co.uk

PRINCE JAKE

He's the Prince of Pranks!

It's Snow Joke!

SUE MONGREDIEN ♛ MARK BEECH

ORCHARD BOOKS

CHAPTER ONE

Splat!

"Gotcha!" Prince Jake guffawed with laughter as his snowball whacked right into his little brother's shoulder.

"Oi!" yelped Prince Ned, fumbling to make his own snowball. And then, seconds later...

Wheeeeee!

Ned had hurled his snowball straight back at Jake, who ducked, still laughing helplessly.

He turned his head to see it thwack against the castle wall and shatter onto the frozen moat behind him.

Jake reached down to scoop up a fresh handful of snow and pack together another freezing missile. The powdery snow squeaked under his gloved fingers, and he grinned broadly. How he loved winter! Snow, sledging, Christmas, school holidays...

"Aim...FIRE!" he yelled, sending the snowball whizzing through the crisp winter air in his brother's direction.

SPLAT!

"Oh, yes!" he chortled as it landed right on Ned's bobble hat, sending it skewing sideways over his eyes. "Bullseye! The hotshot prince hits the target yet again, as he...aargggh!"

A return snowball hit him square in the

chest, thumping against his coat. "Right," he said, "like that, is it?"

For the next few minutes, the two princes flung snowballs back and forth, laughing and panting breathlessly. They were in the snow-covered formal gardens just outside the castle where they lived with their parents, the King and Queen of Morania, and their older sister, Princess Petunia. It wasn't long before both boys were covered in snow, and their toes were starting to go numb inside their wellies. Then, just as Prince Jake had packed together a truly awesome snowball, Ned started waving his arms, an urgent expression on his face. "Over there!" he called in a low voice. "New target sighted!"

Jake turned to look where Ned was pointing – and grinned. Ahh, perfect. Absolutely perfect! There was Princess Petunia crossing the drawbridge, on her way out of the castle. No better target in the world for the fantastic snowball Jake had just made!

He gave it a last bit of patting and shaping, making sure that all the snow was pressed in, and every curve was smooth. It was a beauty!

Princess Petunia was wearing an enormous pink puffa jacket and carrying a pair of ice skates as she walked gingerly over the drawbridge.

9

Prince Jake took very careful aim and fired.
Wheeeeee!
Prince Ned took very careful aim and fired.
Wheeeeee!
SPLAT! SPLAT!
"Aargggh!" Princess Petunia screamed,
as the two snowballs thwacked against
her puffa jacket, and threw up her arms
in fright. She wobbled...and skidded...
and her arms flailed as she tried to keep

her balance. And before Prince Jake
could even cross his fingers that she'd
fall over, her feet were slip-sliding
underneath her and she'd gone flying...
straight off the drawbridge and onto
the frozen moat!

Jake and Ned collapsed with laughter.
Jake thought he might actually fall over
himself, he was laughing so hard. "Perfect!"
he chortled. "Absolutely brilliant!"

"You horrible brats!" screamed Princess Petunia furiously. She scrambled to get onto her hands and knees, the icy moat creaking perilously beneath her weight. "You wait until I…aargggh!"

There was a loud cracking sound and the ice began to break all around her. "Get me out of here!" she bellowed at the top of her voice. "He-e-e-elp!"

♛ ♛ ♛

A short while later, when Jake walked into the royal banqueting hall for Sunday dinner, he couldn't help a slight lurch of dread at the sight that greeted him. There was Princess Petunia, still wrapped in a thermal blanket and shivering theatrically. She gave Jake and Ned looks so evil, Jake was surprised they weren't frazzling the food.

There was King Nicholas – Jake's dad – glaring as if he'd just trapped his big royal bottom in a limousine door.

And, scariest of all, there was Queen Caroline – Jake's mum – with eyes as icy as the moat itself.

Oh no. Oh *help*. He was in big trouble now. Major trouble. Possibly record-breakingly bad, never-been-worse trouble.

"Well, look who it is," Petunia said, through gritted teeth. She was glaring so fiercely at Jake, he half-expected her to start growling like a dog.

He gulped. He'd never seen her look quite so angry before.

"All right?" he mumbled, slipping into his chair and bracing himself for the storm.

"Jacob and Edward," Queen Caroline began, in a voice so frosty it was practically dripping with ice cubes, "I must say, I've been very disappointed with your behaviour over the school holidays."

14

There was a horrible silence. Jake stared at the pristine white tablecloth, wondering which particular offence his mum was going to tell him off for first. Petunia going into the moat was a big one, obviously, but there were a few other teeny tiny things she might have noticed, too...

"The royal racehorses have still not recovered from when you sledged straight into their stable 'by accident'," she said, her voice still on the wrong side of freezing point.

Ahh. Jake had forgotten about that. It had been quite something, the way he'd zoomed along the racetrack at super speed. It wasn't his fault the sledge had no brakes to stop him flying through the stableyard!

"And it was very lucky the Prime Minister could see the funny side of having her briefcase completely filled with snow," the Queen went on.

Jake fiddled with his solid silver teaspoon. Oh yes, the Prime Minister's briefcase. A fantastic idea, that had been. Almost as good as...

"And then there was the *disturbance* at the royal Christmas Ball last week..." The Queen shook her head, her mouth a thin, tight line.

Disturbance? Jake thought. Oh, right. She must be talking about the way he'd livened things up by swapping the music over, so that instead of plinky-plonky piano music drifting through the Great Hall, there had been pounding guitars and drums from the new CD he'd got for Christmas. (But that was *good* music! You could hardly call it a disturbance...)

"Today, however, you've really gone too far. Pushing Petunia into a freezing moat—"

"We didn't *push* her!" Jake corrected,

but his mum silenced him with another chilly glare.

"What were you *thinking*? She could have caught pneumonia!"

"*And* my winter sports coaching starts this week," Petunia put in, almost shrieking with rage. "If I'm too ill to take part, I'll...I'll..." She got to her feet, her fists clenched. "I'll kill you. I mean it!"

"That's enough," the King said sternly. "No killing at the dinner table, please."

17

Jake scowled at the mention of the special coaching that had been arranged for his sister. She'd even been given a week off school – it was so unfair that he wasn't allowed to go along too! "You're too young," his parents had said. "And too naughty. You'll only mess about with the skis and skates, if we let you go…"

Jake had argued, begged and even promised to behave, but they hadn't budged. And so it was that, every day this week, while Petunia was off practising ice-skating and bobsleigh racing and skiing, he and Ned would be stuck in the school room, as usual, having no fun whatsoever. Talk about mean!

"Thank heavens it's the last day of the holidays," the King growled, shooting the boys a severe look from below his bushy eyebrows. "Roll on lessons starting again tomorrow. Maybe then we'll get some peace and quiet around here!"

The Queen picked up her knife and fork,
and Jake crossed his fingers under the table,
hoping that this might mean the lecture
was nearly over. "For your last afternoon of
the holidays, I'd like to set a few rules," she
said. "No more sledging into the stables. No
more snowballing. No trying to skate on the
moat – especially as the ice has all cracked
now. You're meant to be princes! You're
meant to be setting a good example to the
rest of the country!" She sighed. "Boys, just
behave yourselves, that's all I ask. Just stay
out of trouble. All right?"

19

"All right," mumbled Prince Ned, already tucking into his food.

Jake sighed. "All right," he said, although he kept his fingers crossed just in case.

"And stay away from me, too," Petunia hissed. "Because you'll be sorry if you don't!"

Jake waited until his parents weren't looking before he pulled a face at his sister. Her threats didn't scare him – no way. Like she could ever get one over on him!

CHAPTER TWO

As they were finishing their meal, Boris the butler came into the room and gave a bow. "Your Majesties," he said, "I have just been informed that Ms Prudence is suffering from the flu, and will not be able to come in to teach the children tomorrow."

Jake felt a rush of wild joy surge through him. Yes! Oh, yes! Ms Prudence – or the Prune, as she was known to Jake and

Ned – was the royal governess and a dry old stick at the best of times. Jake had not been looking forward to lessons starting again tomorrow. But now…now it seemed as if the school holidays had just got an extension. Talk about a result!

"I have therefore taken the liberty," Boris went on smoothly, before anyone could speak, "of contacting St Augustine's, the nearby prep school, to ask if we could borrow a teacher for the time being."

St Augustine's? Oh, no! Jake's smile vanished. The last time a teacher had come from there on loan, it had been the most horrible man in the world – super-strict and prone to dishing out absolutely masses of homework. Jake shuddered. He could still picture him, with that ferocious gingery moustache and watery blue eyes. What had his name been again?

"Very good, Boris," the Queen said approvingly. "Who are they sending?"

"A chap by the name of Slater," Boris replied. "He's familiar with the castle – he was here last summer when Ms Prudence was on leave."

Slater? Slavedriver Slater? A horrible vision floated into Jake's mind of Mr Slater bellowing at him for muddling up his Moranian history notes, his pale eyes bulging and flecks of spit blasting from underneath that gingery moustache,

23

showering into Jake's face…

Jake dropped his fork, no longer feeling at all hungry. Oh, no! Slavedriver Slater, back at the castle. This was a complete disaster!

A smile seemed to be playing around the King's mouth. "Mr Slater, eh?" he said, looking pleased at the news. "Oh, good. Maybe he will keep you boys in line. Someone's got to, after all!"

Petunia gave a horrible smirk. "And you'll have him all to yourselves, too," she put in. "Because *I'll* be having fun at my sports coaching. What a shame!"

The Queen started discussing speed-skating tactics with Petunia, and the subject moved on from school. Not in Jake's head, though. His mind was still in a frenzy of despair at the terrible news about Mr Slater. He racked his brain frantically. Was there any way he could possibly get out of school for the next week? Hmmm...

He could feign illness. He was an expert at faking coughs and flopping about looking sickly.

Or he could pack up some supplies and hide out for a while. The castle was full of unused rooms and cupboards. It wouldn't be that tricky to stay out of sight until Slavedriver Slater had gone.

He could secretly arrange emergency medical treatment for the Prune, to get her better and back at work as soon as possible.

Or maybe… Jake frowned thoughtfully as another option popped into his head. What if he could somehow prevent Mr Slater from coming to the castle in the first place?

♛ ♛ ♛

"What do you mean? Kidnap him or something? Or…" Ned's eyes were bright with excitement. "Or *poison* him? Or…"

"Well…" Jake looked around carefully as he and his brother went outside after lunch. Good. Nobody in sight who might overhear and tell tales to their parents. "Those aren't bad ideas, but they're a bit…well, drastic."

"How about we send in the Moranian army to surround St Augustine's and refuse to let Mr Slater out of there?" Ned suggested eagerly. "Or…"

Jake shook his head. "No," he interrupted. "It's got to be something subtle. Something simple. Something that won't get us into loads more trouble."

They both fell into thought, trudging along the snowy path. There was silence, save for a faint chugging sound. As they rounded the corner of the castle, Jake saw it was the snow plough, clearing the royal driveway and incoming road of snow. "Shame," he said, pointing it out to Ned. "If we were snowed in, Slater wouldn't be able to get here, would he?"

They both looked up at the sky hopefully, but there wasn't a single snow cloud to be seen, just a sweep of clear blue, with a pale wintry sun shining weakly down.

"Knowing our luck, the snow will have melted by tomorrow," Jake said, feeling gloomy at the thought. "Come on, let's make a snowman while we try to think of a plan."

Jake and Ned got to work. Together, they rolled a ball of snow that was so enormous it took both of them to push it across the lawn.

"Phew," Ned said. "It's going to be a very fat snowman."

"You start on the head," Jake said. "I'll go inside and scrounge a carrot nose from Marco."

Jake ran across the snowy lawn and back into the castle. The royal kitchens were in the southern wing, along with the servants' quarters, and Jake was a frequent visitor there, especially on baking days.

Marco was one of the junior chefs, and he was just taking out a tray of shortbread from the oven when Jake stuck his head around the kitchen door.

"Marco, can I have a carrot, please?" he asked. "Me and Ned are making a snowman."

Marco carefully put down the hot shortbread and took off his oven gloves. "Master Jake, of course!" he said at once, beaming. "One moment, your highness!"

He bustled away and Jake sneaked a little further into the kitchen. He wasn't supposed to go in there – the head chef, Mrs Ambrose, was very strict about that – but the shortbread smelled so sweet and delicious, he just couldn't resist going a bit closer...

"Oi! I've spotted you!"

Oops. There was Mrs Ambrose's shrill

voice, ringing across the room – and here she came now, bustling over, with a floury rolling pin clutched in one hand like a weapon. "'Ow many times, Master Jake? It's 'Elf and Safety, innit? Not allowed in 'ere! Go on – shoo!"

"I'm going, I'm going," Jake said, not actually moving. He had one last reluctant look at the shortbread. How hot was it? he wondered. Would it burn his fingers if he grabbed a piece and ran for it?

"I'll 'ave to tell your mum you've been 'anging around 'ere," Mrs Ambrose threatened, brandishing her rolling pin as she waddled even nearer. "Don't make me tell on you to the Queen, now!"

"All right, all right," Jake grumbled, edging away until he was back in the doorway. "See? I'm out of the kitchen, OK?"

Mrs Ambrose nodded in a satisfied sort of a way, her chins rippling with creases as she did so, and returned to her pastry. Marco reappeared seconds later with a huge knobbly carrot, which he slipped to Jake. Then, with a sympathetic wink, he cut some shortbread, wrapped it in foil, and slid it along the worktop for Jake to catch.

"So, you're making a snowman, eh?" he asked. He pointed to his white chef's hat. "Not tempted to make a snow chef? I could lend you a hat and apron if you want."

Out of the corner of his eye, Jake could see portraits of his parents up on the kitchen wall. His gaze rested wonderingly upon his dad's face for a moment, and then he turned back to Marco. "No, you're all right, cheers," he said with a grin. "I've just had a better idea."

He shoved the carrot and shortbread
into his pocket. "Thanks, Marco," he said.
"See you later!"

Then, still grinning, he headed away
from the kitchen. Not back outside to
where Ned was, though. Not yet. First, he
had a couple of things to collect from his
parents' bedroom...

CHAPTER THREE

A little while later, the snowman was
finished. He was enormous. He had
a fat round belly, a big orange nose,
thick bushy eyebrows (made from tree
bark), twiggy brown hair and black
pebble eyes.

Over his snowy body and skinny branch
arms, he wore a rich red dining jacket,
embroidered with golden thread around
the cuffs and collar, and with a golden

crown emblem on one pocket. A belt held
the jacket around his portly belly. On his
head he wore a bejewelled crown that
glinted in the sunlight.

Jake and Ned couldn't stop giggling.
"This is the funniest snow king ever,"
Ned said, patting on some moss to make
a hairy chest sticking out above the
jacket. "What else can we put on him to
make him look like Dad?"

Jake thought for a moment. "Maybe
a big medallion," he suggested, chuckling.
He fished in his pocket for the tin
foil Marco had sneaked him. The
shortbread had long gone, but maybe
he could shape the foil into some kind
of chain...

"And he could be holding some food,"
Ned added. "A pie or something. You
know what a greedy-guts Dad is."

"Good idea," Jake agreed. "Go and see

if Marco will give you anything."

Jake busily moulded the foil into a thick silver chain, complete with a large silver medallion dangling from it. He hung it around the snow king's plump white neck, while Ned went off to the kitchen.

"What is *that*?" came a voice just then, and Jake turned to see Petunia approaching, carrying her skates. "Is it meant to be Dad?"

"Yeah," Jake said. "Good, isn't it?"

"Mmmm," Petunia said thoughtfully. She seemed to have forgotten all about the moat incident now, luckily. She took her mobile phone out of her coat pocket and snapped a picture. "Hey, tell you what, why don't you go and stand next to it and I'll take a photo?" she suggested. "You could do something funny, like stick your tongue out at it."

Jake laughed. "Yeah, all right," he said. He went over and did a few silly poses – sticking his tongue out at the snow king, tweaking its nose, poking it in the belly and pretending to kick it.

"That's perfect," Petunia said, slipping her phone back in her pocket. "They'll love this," she added with a smile.

"What?" Jake asked, overhearing. There was something about Petunia's smile that suddenly made him suspicious.

"You're going to show Mum and Dad?"

Petunia wrinkled her nose. "As if I'd do a mean thing like that!" she scoffed. "No, I'll just show some…friends. Anyway, gotta go. See you later!"

She walked away, her fingers flying nimbly over the keypad on her phone. She was probably texting the photo to one of her simpering mates, Jake thought, losing interest. Big deal!

A few moments later, he heard the chugging noise again and turned to see the snow plough trundling up the castle driveway, steered by Mr Mackintosh, one of the handymen. Jake's shoulders slumped as he remembered how Mr Slater would be driving up to the castle tomorrow morning. Rats! Why did the school holidays have to be so *short*? If he ever became king, he'd make it the law that children got a whole month off every

Christmas, and at least three months off
in the summer. As for spit-showering,
goggle-eyed, arm-waving teachers – well,
they'd be thrown to the wolves. How the
children of Morania would all love
him for it!

He watched as Mr Mackintosh guided
the snow plough towards one of the royal
garages, turned off the engine and
jumped down from the cab. Jake waited
until he'd disappeared into the castle

before wading through the deep snow down to the garages for a better look. The snow plough was yellow and shiny, with snow still clinging to the front shovel.

That was when Jake had his brilliant idea. If the snow plough could clear the snow *off* the road...then surely it was perfectly capable of shovelling it back *onto* the road...

And if there was lots of snow on the road, then Mr Slater wouldn't be able to drive to the castle...

And if Mr Slater wasn't able to drive to the castle, there'd be no lessons!

Jake grinned and hopped up into the cab of the plough. Sometimes he was a genius! And, by a stroke of luck, Mr Mackintosh had left the engine key dangling from the ignition...

Jake looked carefully at the dashboard. Was he really going to do this? Did he dare? The controls all seemed simple enough. There was a silver lever marked "Forwards" and "Backwards". There was another lever to lift and lower the shovel. There was a steering wheel. There were switches marked "Headlights". No problem. It couldn't have been more straightforward!

All he had to do now was decide whether he had the guts to give it a go…

A memory of Mr Slater looming at the blackboard like a rubbery-mouthed, pop-eyed monster slammed into Jake's head. He gave a queasy shudder and tried to shake the image from his mind's eye. Right. Decision made. No question!

Jake took a deep breath and turned the key. A loud chugging started up from the engine and the vibration made his seat judder. His heart pounding with his own daring, he pushed the lever to the "Forwards" position. For a split second, he thought nothing was going to happen, but then the snow plough made a mighty rumbling noise and began rolling forwards along the path.

"How cool is this!" Jake breathed, grinning to himself. "Here we go!"

Chugga-chugga-chugga-chugga…

Jake turned the gigantic steering wheel
to guide the snow plough around, then set
off towards the road. He couldn't get over
how high up he was as the huge wheels
rumbled along. He figured he might
as well go a good distance down the
drive – after all, if Mr Slater was able to
get too near the castle in his car before the
road was blocked, he'd be able to walk
the rest of the distance. No – Jake didn't
want that. Far better to block the end of

the long castle drive. That way Mr Slater
would be forced to give up before he'd
even arrived!

Chugga-chugga-chugga-chugga…

Jake was getting the hang of this now.
There was nothing to it! All he had to do
was keep the wheel steady, and the plough
just rumbled along nicely. Easy! He even
tried a few swerves to left and right, just to
keep things interesting. *Whooosh! Whoosh!*

Snow sprayed up on either side as he took the plough to the edges of the drive. This was brilliant fun!

A few minutes later, he'd reached the end of the road. Mr Mackintosh had done a thorough job, pushing the snow far off the tarmac so that it was banked up at the sides. *OK*, thought Jake. *Time to start shovelling it all back on the road again!*

He turned the snow plough so that it sat sideways on the road and reached for the shovel control. Lower...scoop...lift...swing it round...and drop!

Bingo!

Once he got the hang of the controls, Jake worked quickly, shovelling piles and piles of snow across the road until it was completely covered. He had to reverse as he went, so as not to get himself blocked in, but that was easy enough. This was definitely one of his best ideas yet. He was already imagining with glee how Boris would break the news tomorrow morning:

"Just had a call from Mr Slater...terribly sorry but he won't be able to make it after all...road completely blocked... dreadful shame..."

Jake laughed out loud. "Dreadful shame? I don't think so," he said to himself. "Party time, more like!"

He drove the snow plough back to the garages and switched off the engine. Nobody was around. He'd actually got away with it!

👑 👑 👑

The next morning, as Jake was approaching the breakfast room, he could hear his dad's shocked voice booming out of the door. "No! I can't believe it! I just can't believe it!"

Jake pricked up his ears. This sounded interesting. What was going on? he wondered. Had Slavedriver phoned already?

He could hear the Queen's voice next, making soothing murmuring noises.

"But it's on the front page of every single one!" the King burst out. "I'll be the laughing stock of the whole country!"

Jake stepped up his pace, dying to know what the King was talking about. *Why* was he in all the newspapers? *Why* would he be the laughing stock of the whole country? Whatever this was about, it sounded big.

He went into the breakfast room to see his dad, scarlet in the face, surrounded by piles of newspapers. "Ahh, here he is!" the King said, holding one of them up in the air. He seemed to bristle at the very sight of Jake. "Is this anything to do with you, son?"

Jake stared. And stared. Uh-oh. His heart sank right down into his shoes. Oh, no....

On the front page of the newspaper there was a picture of him, Jake, posing next to the snow king. "FREEZE A JOLLY GOOD FELLOW!" the headline read.

"I…" Jake stammered. This was Petunia's doing – he knew it! Stitched up by Petunia! Sure, he'd known she was mad with him, but he hadn't realised just how mad. "I…"

"Here's another one," the King snapped, holding up a second newspaper. "ICE TO SEE YOU!" the headline shouted, under a picture of Jake tweaking the snow king's nose. "And another. And…well, they've all got these pictures. All of them! What were you *thinking*?"

CHAPTER FOUR

Jake looked down at his feet and
shuffled them round a bit. "Well, I..."
he began – but just then, Princess Petunia
bustled in past him, her jewellery clinking
and jangling as she walked.

"Morning, Mum, morning, Dad – oh!"
She stopped as she saw the newspaper
front pages.

"Yes," the King said bitterly. "Oh, indeed.
I'm going to be the joke of Morania. How

will anyone take me seriously again?" He tossed the newspapers to the floor and sank his head into his hands.

Petunia picked up one of them and read the caption. "His Royal Ice-ness King Nicholas, looking a little frosty, as sculpted by his son, Prince Jake." She smirked at Jake in a horrible, gloating way. "Oh dear, Jake. Naughty, naughty!"

Jake made a lunge for Petunia, but Queen Caroline grabbed him by the scruff of the neck before he could get to her. "You did this!" Jake yelled at his sister. "You took those photos!"

"I don't know *what* you're talking about," Petunia said lightly, sticking her tongue out at him when nobody was looking. "I was practising my skating yesterday afternoon – once I'd warmed up from being pushed into the freezing moat, that is."

"Oh, I get it," Jake spat. "This is you getting a bit of revenge, isn't it? Well, you just wait! I'll…"

"Jake! Petunia! That's quite enough!" the Queen interrupted, in her fiercest voice.

Silence fell, interrupted only by Boris appearing in the room. "Sorry to interrupt, your Majesties, but I've just had a call from Mr Slater," he said, with a curious glance across at Jake. "He says he's unable to get to the castle this morning – apparently the road is quite blocked."

Jake sat down, trying not to look
triumphant.

"Blocked?" the Queen echoed, sounding
puzzled. "But I only gave orders for it to be
cleared yesterday. And it hasn't snowed in
that time. What's the problem?"

Boris gave a delicate cough. "The snow
plough was sent out yesterday, you're quite
right, your Majesty," he said. "But it seems
there is again some kind of blockage there
now." He sent another glance in Jake's
direction. Jake pretended not to notice.

"I will make sure the road is cleared once again," Boris continued. "In the meantime, would you like me to arrange for another teacher to come in?"

The Queen sighed. "Until the road's clear, there's no point," she said. "And it's too short notice to get anyone else now anyway. But ask him to come back tomorrow, please, Boris. We'll make sure there's not a flake of snow on the road by then." She eyed Jake. "In the meantime, it looks like there's no school after all."

No school! Jake just loved it when a plan worked out the way it was supposed to. And this one had turned out absolutely perfectly!

Now all he needed to do was get Petunia back for those photos. He thought hard as he ate his crownflakes, barely tasting them. Maybe he could try to take a photo of *her* looking stupid, he thought to himself.

Email *that* off to the newspapers, just as
Petunia must have done. He was sure
they'd love it. Even better, he was sure that
vain Petunia would absolutely *hate* it.

After breakfast, Petunia went to get ready
for her first day of sports school, while the
Queen sent Jake and Ned to play outside.
"The Prime Minister's flying in today, with
some other very important people, and
I don't want you getting in the way," she
said. Her eyebrows knotted together as
she gave Jake a warning look. "And
I certainly don't want any more snow
ending up in the Prime Minister's
briefcase, thank you very much. Off
you go!"

Jake didn't mind being sent outside at
all. In fact, it fitted in nicely with his plan
to get Petunia back. He'd decided that he
would make loads and loads of super-hard

snowballs and then, once he'd got a good collection together, he'd launch an attack on her. He would pelt her with them mercilessly, and then, when she was totally covered in snow, hair plastered to her head, he'd take a photo of her. Ha! That would teach her.

Ned was looking excited about something as they put on their coats and hats, ready to head outside. "I'm going to have a go on that snow plough," he said in a low voice. "It sounded really good fun. Will you show me how to work it?"

Jake shook his head. "I've got to get Petunia first," he said, patting the pocket where he'd put his camera. He slung an empty bag over his shoulder, smiling to himself at the thought of filling it with snowballs. "It's dead easy to drive the snow plough, though," he added. "All you do is turn the key and push the lever to go forwards."

The boys went outside and Ned ran off to where the snow plough was parked outside the garages, the place Jake had left it the day before. Jake, meanwhile, could see Petunia coming out of the castle, obviously intending to make her way to the royal heliport. She was getting flown out to Mount Morania for her first skiing lesson, the lucky thing. But before she could do any of that, Jake was determined to have his revenge. Right! Now to make a few snowballs!

He got to work, rolling and patting and shaping the snow until he had twenty or so snowballs in his bag. Oh-ho! This lot would have Petunia totally covered. She'd be sorry she ever tried to pull a fast one on the mighty Prince Jake!

Just as he was about to set off after her, though, he heard a rumbling sound. Then he heard a shout. He turned around to see the snow plough chugging along on its own – and there was Ned running frantically after it!

"I fell out of the side!" Ned wailed, puffing along behind the snow plough. "Help, Jake! Help me stop it!"

Chugga-chugga-chugga-chugga...

The snow plough was too far away for Jake to be able to catch it. It was trundling along at quite a speed, heading straight for the royal lake – and Petunia, who was right in its path!

Jake's eyes widened in shock. Hadn't Petunia heard the snow plough's engine? Why wasn't she getting out of the way?

"Petunia!" he yelled. "Hey – look behind you!"

Petunia didn't seem to hear that, either. Was she ignoring him?

Chugga-chugga-chugga-chugga...

"She's got her headphones on!" Ned noticed. "She can't hear anything except her music!"

It was true, Jake realised. Petunia was bobbing her head in time to a tune as she walked along. *That* was why she couldn't hear the snow plough, or their shouts!

Chugga-chugga-chugga-chugga...

Jake thought quickly. The snow plough was getting nearer and nearer his sister. If it hit her, it would surely break every bone in her body. It might even kill her. And even though he wanted to get her back for the snow king photo, he didn't want revenge *that* badly.

But he was too far from the snow plough to stop it. He was too far from Petunia to warn her. There was only one thing to be done. He grabbed a snowball from his bag, took careful aim and fired...

Wheeeeee!

SPLAT!

Jake's aim was as accurate as always. The snowball hit Petunia smartly on the head – dislodging her headphones.

"Oi!" she squealed, turning around and glaring.

"Get out of the way!" Jake and Ned both bellowed, running towards her.

They saw Petunia's face whiten as she realised the snow plough was heading straight for her. In a few seconds, it would plough right into her, crushing her to a princessy pulp!

"Aargggh!" she screamed, diving out of the way.

FLUMP. She landed in a huge bank of snow and her body completely disappeared from view as she sank into it.

Chugga-chugga-chugga-chugga…
CRASH! SPLASH!

The snow plough rumbled on, straight into the frozen lake, where it smashed through the ice and plunged into the water. There was a loud hissing sound, and smoke poured out of its engine, then it disappeared under the water with a few bubbles, and finally went silent.

CHAPTER FIVE

Jake and Ned ran over to Petunia. She was staggering to her feet, absolutely covered from head to foot in snow. She had snow in her hair, snow in her eyelashes, snow in her ears and all over her clothes.

Snap!

Snap!

Snap!

Jake took out his camera and clicked

a few photos before she could brush any of it off. Then he remembered to say, "Are you all right?"

Petunia was looking rather dazed, and kept staring around in bewilderment. "Where... Where did it go?" she asked, blinking the snow from her eyes.

"It's in the lake," Jake said, pointing to the massive hole in the ice, where bubbles were still rising to the surface.

Ned looked as if he were about to cry at what he'd done. "Sorry," he said in a small voice. "It was an accident, I promise. I just thought I'd have a go on it for a laugh, but when I tried to reach the steering wheel, my arms weren't long enough, and then I fell off the seat and out of the side, and..."

Petunia wiped the snow from her face, still looking shell-shocked. "You just...saved my *life*..." she said, sounding amazed.

"Jake – you actually saved my life. That thing would have completely flattened me!"

Jake shrugged, trying to look as if saving his sister's life was an everyday kind of event. "I suppose I did," he said. He grinned. "Saved by a snowball!"

The King and Queen came running out of the castle then, followed by the Prime Minister, Boris and several other members of staff. "We heard the crash!" the King panted, his crown slipping on his head as

he ran through the snow. "Is everyone all right?"

"What happened?" the Queen called, her long velvet dress getting snow all over its hem. "Is anybody hurt?"

Princess Petunia stepped forwards, her lower lip quivering. "Jake just saved my life," she said dramatically. "He's a hero! And… And I owe him an apology, too. It was me who sent the photos of the snow king to the newspapers. I'm really sorry, Daddy."

The full story came out then. Ned was sent to his bedroom in disgrace for trashing the snow plough. Petunia was in big trouble for leaking the photos to the press, and letting Jake take the blame for them. And Jake? Jake was hugged and praised over and over again for his quick-thinking, and perfect aim.

"You know, son, you're such a good shot with those snowballs, I bet you'll be a brilliant bowler," the King said happily as they went back inside. "I'll have to

book you in for a cricket summer camp,
get you a few weeks off school so that
you can have some special coaching.
You're a natural, I'm sure!"

Jake beamed in delight. Cricket
summer camp? A few weeks off school?
"That would be great, Dad," he said.
"Thanks."

The next morning, the royal family were
all over the newspapers again – but it
wasn't pictures of the snow king that
had been printed this time.

"PRINCE JAKE SAVES THE DAY!"
declared one headline, with a story
about Jake saving Petunia from the
runaway snow plough.

"MORANIAN CRICKET CAPTAIN IN
THE MAKING?" pondered a second
newspaper, with a huge picture of Jake
clutching a snowball.

But Jake's favourite front pages were the ones that had published his photos of Petunia covered in snow.

"PRINCESS ATCHOO-NIA," said one.

"THE ABOMINABLE SNOW PRINCESS!" said another.

"IT'S SNOW JOKE FOR PRINCESS PETUNIA," said a third.

Oh yes, thought Jake to himself, as he snipped out the photos of his sister for safe-keeping. He had the feeling she wouldn't be playing any tricks on him for quite some time...

LOOK OUT FOR MORE
RIGHT ROYAL LAUGHS WITH

Sticky Gum Fun
978 1 84616 618 1   £3.99

It's Snow Joke!
978 1 84616 614 3   £3.99

Dungeon of Doom
978 1 84616 617 4   £3.99

Knighty-Knight
978 1 84616 613 6   £3.99

Monster Madness
978 1 84616 615 0   £3.99

Swordfights and Slimeballs!
978 1 84616 616 7   £3.99

Here's a taster of

Dungeon
of Doom

It was a Friday lunchtime in the castle of
Morania, and everyone around the royal
dining table was deep in thought.

Prince Jake was plotting. He and Prince
Ned had been trying to catch rats last
night, down by the dungeons. Jake
was really hoping they could get one
to sneak into Princess Petunia's
four-poster bed. It would be so funny!

Prince Ned was excited. He couldn't wait
for PE that afternoon. The captain of the
Moranian national football team, Hat-Trick
Haywood, was visiting the castle to give the

royal children a special training session.
How cool was that?!

Princess Petunia was daydreaming. She
was imagining herself scoring the winning
goal in the annual Toffs versus Town polo
match tomorrow. She and her mum were
in the Toffs team, along with "Gorgeous"
George Barrington, the Duke of Bentley's
son. "Oh, Petunia," she hoped George
would say. "You were fabulous!"

King Nicholas was licking his lips. Would
it be really greedy of him to have another
spoonful of roast potatoes? "Well, I am
King, after all," he muttered to himself,
signalling to Boris, the butler, that he would
like more. "And kings get to do whatever
they want!"

Queen Caroline was fretting. She'd lost
her best bracelet, which had been in the
Moranian royal family for years. It was
solid silver, and clipped together with a little

hinge. She always wore it to polo matches as a lucky charm, but it seemed to have vanished.

"Boys, you haven't seen my silver bracelet anywhere, have you?" she said at that moment, gazing over the dining table at her sons.

Prince Jake pretended to be chewing a tough bit of roast goose, while he thought about what to say. He certainly wasn't going to tell the truth! If his mum knew that he and Ned had been using her precious bracelet as part of a rat lasso they'd made, she'd have a right royal fit!

Prince Ned, who was younger than Jake and a lot less sneakier, piped up. "We were playing with it near the dungeons," he said, "and—"

Jake kicked him under the table and shot him a warning look. "He means, we were taking it to be polished for you, and went past the dungeons," he fibbed, in his most innocent voice. "And—"

Prince Ned let out a snigger. "And then Jake got scared because we thought we heard the ghost, and we ran away, and—"

"I was not scared!" Jake interrupted indignantly. "YOU were scared, more like. And anyway, it was only that door banging which made me jump a bit. There's no way I'm scared of ghosts..."

PICK UP A COPY OF

Dungeon of Doom

TO FIND OUT WHAT HAPPENS NEXT!